SPACE  PIRATES

Stranded!

There was a huge flash as something disappeared behind a gigantic asteroid. Sam watched the asteroid closely.

"Oh no, it can't be," he said. But it was. "It's *Gravity's Revenge*! Black-Hole Beard is coming!"

Look out for more
stories of swashbuckling
space adventures in

Stowaway!

Mutiny!

Treasure!

SPACE PIRATES

Stranded!

JIM LADD

Illustrated by
Benji Davies

nosy
crow

With special thanks to Paul Harrison
To Sam — the pirate who completed the crew

First published in the UK in 2013 by Nosy Crow Ltd,
The Crow's Nest, 10a Lant Street, London SE1 1QR, UK

Nosy Crow and associated logos are trademarks and/or registered
trademarks of Nosy Crow Ltd

Text © Hothouse Fiction, 2013
Illustrations © Benji Davies, 2013

The right of Hothouse Fiction to be identified as the author of this work
has been asserted by them in accordance with the Copyright, Designs and
Patents Act, 1988

1 3 5 7 9 10 8 6 4 2

A CIP catalogue record for this book is available from the British Library

Printed and bound in the UK by Clays Ltd, St Ives Plc

Papers used by Nosy Crow are made from wood grown in sustainable forests.

ISBN: 978 0 85763 211 1

www.nosycrow.com

Who's who in
COMET'S CREW

SAM
STARBUCK

CAPTAIN COMET

BARNEY

PEGG
AND
LEGG

Who's who in
BLACK-HOLE BEARD'S CREW

BAGGOT

YARR

BLACK-HOLE
BEARD

"Full speed ahead!" Sam yelled.

The large sails of the spaceship *Jolly Apollo* filled with solar winds and tacked gracefully across the empty space of the Auroran solar system. The *Jolly Apollo* was no ordinary spaceship – it was a pirate ship! It was also a patched-up wreck, crewed by an assorted bunch of aliens who were quite possibly the most useless space pirates the galaxy had ever seen. All apart from one: the new cabin boy, Samson Starbuck.

"That's it! That's Lumiere Max!" said Sam, pointing at a nearby sun.

"Batten your hatch there, shipmate. Some of us are trying to get a well-earned rest," replied Captain Comet.

Comet was the captain of the *Apollo*. He was tall, thin and three-eyed (though eye patches covered two of his eyes), with a magnificent waxed moustache. Dressed in a long frock coat and tricorn hat, he looked every inch the perfect pirate. Unfortunately, Comet's dress-sense was the most pirate-like thing about him. At that precise moment he was lounging in a chair with a pair of three-lensed sunglasses perched on his nose and a foaming glass of grum in his hand.

Grum was the drink of choice for pirates – a kind of foamy lemonade that encouraged singing and kept space-scurvy away.

"But Captain," Sam insisted, "Lumiere Max is on my parents' map!"

Sam's parents had been spaceship-wrecked on the legendary Planet X, but had managed to use their ship's homing beacon to send Sam a map, scribbled on a piece of spacesuit material.

The little planet where Sam and his parents lived was a barren rock in the middle of nowhere, with nothing on it apart from his parent's lab and a port full of vicious space pirates. Luckily, the only thing space pirates love more than bowling is treasure, and every pirate had heard the rumours about Planet X – a lost planet made of solid gold. When Sam had shown Captain Comet the map, he'd been welcomed aboard as the newest member of the *Jolly Apollo*'s crew.

"Lumiere Max? Are you sure?" asked Comet, suddenly interested.

He fished around inside his coat and pulled out the scrap of silvery spacesuit material the map was drawn on. Pushing his sunglasses up on to his head he peered at it intently. He blinked, and then – making sure no one was looking – flicked up his eye-patches to reveal two perfectly good eyes. He stared again at the map.

"Well, blow down me main braces, that's right!" Comet muttered to himself. He flipped his patches back down and cleared his throat. "Well done, Sam. I wondered when you'd spot it. I'd noticed it myself ages ago, of course."

Across the deck, Barney the ship's cook – a huge squid-like alien – grinned and rolled his eyes at Comet's boastful ways. Barney was using a curved mirror to barbeque some disgusting-looking fishy lumps in the heat of the sun.

"Right-ho! Pegg, Legg – plot a course to the centre of that sun," said Comet to his two-headed first mate.

"Aye, aye, sir!" replied Legg, the happy head.

"Are you quite sure about that, Cap'n?" Pegg, the grumpy one, asked warily.

"Yes, yes, quite sure," said Comet.

"Of course he's sure!" Legg told his other head.

"'Of course he's sure'," Pegg replied in a sing-song voice, mocking Legg.

"I think Pegg might have a point," said Sam, looking over Comet's shoulder at the map. "I mean, if you get too close to a star like Lumiere Max the heat would melt a ship like this, wouldn't it? Yes, look, you've got the map upside down."

"What are you talking about?" snapped Comet, spinning the map around and looking at it at different angles. "Oh well! I mean, there you go – clearly we shouldn't be going into the sun! Pegg, Legg – set a course *away* from the sun and towards the Corkscrew Galaxy. Honestly! If only your mother could write properly, Samson!" Comet flicked his sunglasses back down and dropped huffily into his deck chair.

Sam shook his head and did his best to try and

ignore the dreadful smell wafting from Barney's barbeque. Perhaps missing lunch today would be a good idea.

Around him the alien crew of the *Apollo* swung into action as the ship changed course. Lines were hauled to adjust the sails high above Sam's head.

"A little help here, shipmate," called one of the crew and Sam dashed over to lend a hand, wrapping one of the great ropes around a bollard on the side of the deck rails. At the back of the hull, rocket boosters rumbled into life as the spaceship increased speed.

Suddenly Captain Comet sat bolt upright and clutched at his moustache, which was quivering like the tail of a Vaporian Tremble Hound. Sam had seen this once before, back on the planet Jungrum when a grumigator was about to attack. Comet's twitching face fuzz meant only one thing – danger!

"Is everything OK, Captain?" asked Sam.

"I think so," said Comet doubtfully. "It's probably just Barney's cooking. I mean there's nothing to see out there."

He waved airily at the emptiness of space around them.

"Right then, me hearties," said Comet, getting up. "It's going to be a while before we get to the Corkscrew Galaxy – what say we have a game of bowling while we wait?"

The crew cheered enthusiastically. Sam hadn't met a space pirate yet who didn't love to bowl. The crew started to head down to the below-deck bowling alley. Sam waited as they filed downstairs. From where he was he could hear the sound of pirates emptying their

lockers and sea chests for their bowling shoes. Sam was just about to follow them when he noticed Pegg and Legg fighting over a telescope.

"I had it first!" shouted Legg.

"You couldn't see a space haddock if it was slapping you in the face!" snapped Pegg. "Here, give it to me!"

"What in the name of Quark are you two arguing about now?" called Comet, sticking his head back up the stairway.

"I thought I saw something," replied Legg.

"And I was going to check!" said Pegg, trying to wrestle the telescope away.

"Let me have a look," said Sam, gently prising the telescope from the first mate.

Sam scanned the space around him, but there was nothing to be seen but stars, moons, asteroids and the hazy mists of a distant nebula. Sam swung the telescope past the bright glow of rocket boosters – and stopped. *Hang on* – rocket boosters? He looked again, but there was nothing there. Then there was a flash as something disappeared behind a gigantic asteroid. Sam increased the magnification and watched the asteroid closely.

There was another flash of rocket booster as a spaceship scuttled across to another hiding place behind another, closer asteroid.

"Oh no, it can't be," said Sam, a deep sense of dread shivering through him. But it was.

"It's the *Gravity's Revenge*! Black-Hole Beard is coming!"

Chapter Two
GRAVITY'S REVENGE

Black-Hole Beard was the meanest, fiercest, most ruthless pirate to sail the seven galaxies. He had always bullied, mocked and generally trampled all over Captain Comet and the *Jolly Apollo*, until Sam joined the crew. Black-Hole Beard had already tried to steal the map to Planet X, and would have got away with it if Sam hadn't swapped the grum bottle containing the map for an empty one. Now Black-Hole Beard was out for revenge!

"By Neptune's beard!" shouted Comet in a panic. "Are you sure? Quick – hide the grum! All hands on deck! Splice the main wheel! Polish the anchor! Twist the yard arm!"

"I think the captain's having one of his panic attacks," muttered one of the crew.

"Perhaps one of my Flugel Squid kebabs might help," said Barney, lifting a slimy-looking mess in one of his tentacles.

"Your cooking is never the answer," sneered Pegg. "Not unless the question is: 'what's the only thing in the Universe that's more disgusting

than a vomit worm?'"

"Barney tries his best!" cried Legg, the nicer of the two heads.

"Hold on," said Sam. "I don't think he's trying to catch us."

"What's that?" said Comet, peering from around the main mast.

Sam fiddled with the settings on the telescope and looked again.

"Nope, he's definitely keeping the same distance away – I think he's trying to *follow us* to Planet X."

"No one outsmarts Captain Joseph Hercules Invictus Comet!" shouted the *Jolly Apollo*'s captain. "Right-ho, me hearties, set those rocket boosters to maximum and let's get out of here."

"Hold on a minute, Captain," said Sam. "If we run now they'll just follow us. But they don't know that *we* know what they're up to. Why don't we wait until they're behind a particularly big asteroid and then hit the accelerator? It might give us a bit of a head start."

"Just what I was going to say," said Comet, but even he couldn't help blushing a little at the lie. "Well done, Sam. I can see you're learning quickly under my expert guidance. OK, crew, stand by!"

For a few nail-biting minutes, Sam and the crew watched as *Gravity's Revenge* slunk up behind them. As it edged behind a particularly large chunk of space rock, Sam called out to Comet. "OK, Captain, they're out of sight."

"Mr Piole, hard to port! Mr Vulpus, maximum thrust!" Comet shouted.

The *Apollo* lurched forwards and then stopped, the engines backfired and then they were off again.

"Full sail ahead!" yelled Comet.

Everything was rattling so hard that Sam's teeth juddered. He gripped on to the shaking deck rail for support as the ship jerked up and down as if it was about to fall apart. Worst of all, they still seemed to be travelling quite slowly.

"Iiiiiiisssss thiiiisssss iiiiiittttttt?" he asked, the rattling ship bouncing the words from his mouth.

"Whhaaaaattttt?" said Comet.

"Issss thisss assss fassstt assss ttthe *Appppollllllo* goesssss?"

Comet gave the main mast a sharp kick and the shaking stopped.

"We are actually travelling at speeds so fast they are beyond your planet-lubber's imagination. Inexperience is deceiving your eyes, my boy," Comet replied grandly.

He patted the mast proudly, which immediately set the ship off shaking again. Quickly Comet slapped the ship and the rattling ceased. He stared off into the distance pretending nothing had happened.

"Hmmm," Sam replied, watching a shoal of surprised-looking Gaspasian space fish overtake them. Gaspasian space fish were famous for being so round they looked like balloons. They were also famous for being incredibly slow.

"Ha! This is the life," said Comet, clapping Sam on the back. "Tearing through the galaxies, outwitting your enemies – the life of a space pirate is a grand one indeed! I wonder how long

it'll be before that numbskull Black-Hole Beard realises we've got away?''

KKKEEEERRRBBBOOOOOOOMMMM! A flash from a laser cannon tore across the *Apollo*'s deck. Everyone ducked as the laserball skimmed over their heads and exploded.

"I guess they've worked it out!" shouted Sam as he grabbed a telescope. He quickly zoomed in on *Gravity's Revenge,* which was in hot pursuit. "Yep, they're on our tail."

"Would you look at that!" said Comet indignantly, holding up his tricorn hat. There was a huge smoking scorch hole where the laser blast had cut through it. "My second-best hat! Mr Zlit, please bring my third-best hat from my cabin – it's just been promoted. Sheesh! Any lower and it would have hit me square in the face. Oh my... I feel a little faint."

Comet staggered over to the main mast and slid down it into an unconscious heap.

KKKEEEERRRBBBOOOOOOOMMMM!

Another laser cannon blast ripped across the bows of the *Apollo.* Sam knew they needed to do something – and fast!

"Piole, hard to starboard!" Sam shouted.

The *Jolly Apollo* lurched to the right, just as another laserball exploded into the space where they had just been.

18

"Piole, keep zigzagging!" Sam shouted.

"That's right, Mr Teddy, that's right," muttered Captain Comet in his sleep, before rolling over on his side and sucking his thumb.

Another blast flashed across the deck, slicing through some of the rigging. The ropes snapped in the breeze with a crack like a laser musket. The noise was enough to wake the collapsed captain.

"What's going on?" asked Comet, groggily, as he struggled to his feet.

"Everything's under control, Captain," said Sam. "For the moment, anyway."

Suddenly the large on-deck holoscreen flickered into life. The face of Black-Hole Beard loomed large over the *Apollo*'s crew. A huge, thick black beard covered most of his face and was tied in tight bunches. Above the grizzled beard, two small black eyes burned with fury. On Black-Hole Beard's shoulder sat Baggot, his strange bird-like companion.

"Here we go," sighed Comet, as he watched the flickering image. "I wish I was still unconscious."

"Comet! Comet, you mangy sea urchin! I'm coming to get you, you lily-livered son of a space cow!" bellowed Black-Hole Beard.

"Cawr! Cawr! Slowest Comet in the Universe!" squawked Baggot.

"That's right, me beauty," said Black-Hole Beard. "There's nowhere to run to, and there's nowhere you can hide!"

"Your ship is too slow,

And there's nowhere to go! Cawr," sang Baggot.

"I'm coming for that map, Comet," snarled Black-Hole Beard, "and when I get it, you're FINISHED!"

Chapter Three
THE NEBULA

Captain Comet cowered in a ball on the deck. He looked as if he was trying to fold his lanky limbs as far as possible inside his hat, like a squid trying to squeeze itself into a bean can.

"He's right," Comet whimpered. "The *Revenge* is much faster than us – we can't outrun it. We're just going to have to hand over the map. If we stop now he might be merciful. He'll probably steal all our grum again, but I can live with that."

"No!" shouted Sam. He wasn't going to surrender the map to the evil pirate captain – the fate of his parents was resting on it. Besides, he wasn't going to let Comet be pushed around by Black-Hole Beard.

"We don't have to give the map up," Sam continued. "We can't run, but we *can* hide – look!" Sam pointed into the distance. Ahead of them was a nebula, a gigantic misty cloud where stars were made.

"That looks big enough to lose a dozen galaxies

inside, never mind a spaceship," said Sam.

"By Pluto's moons, you're right," said Comet. "Pegg, Legg, do we have enough speed in the old girl to get us there before the *Revenge*?"

"They say 'tis bad luck to cross a nebula," grumbled Pegg.

"Aye, you're right there, shipmate," replied Legg, agreeing with his other head for once.

"It'd be very unlucky to stay here!" said Sam as another laser cannon streaked across their bows.

"Do we have enough speed to get there?" Comet demanded.

The first mate checked the instruments, had a quick argument between its heads, hit the instrument panel with a fist then checked the readings again.

"Aye, aye, Cap'n, we reckon we do," they replied. "But, Captain—"

"Come *on*, Captain," Sam urged.

Comet looked from his first mate to his cabin boy and back again. Another cannon blast finally made his mind up for him. He nodded at Sam.

"Zlit, set a course for that nebula!" Sam shouted to the crocodile-headed alien that was steering the *Apollo*.

"And make it snappy!" said Comet. "Emergency thrust!"

The *Jolly Apollo* lurched violently in the direction of the nebula, its engines whining under the strain. The sudden increase in speed seemed to catch *Gravity's Revenge* by surprise – Sam guessed that most ships just surrendered

when Black-Hole Beard was chasing them, but the *Jolly Apollo* was streaking away.

From the *Apollo*, the crew could see the *Revenge*'s rocket boosters firing into overdrive. But it was too little, too late. Even though *Gravity's Revenge* was the biggest, fastest pirate ship in the galaxy and the *Jolly Apollo* was a clapped-out barge of a ship, there was nothing Black-Hole Beard could do about it. The *Jolly Apollo* was getting away.

"Ha ha! Eat my stardust, Beardy!" shouted Comet.

He leaned against the ship's rails next to Sam and they both looked at the fast-approaching nebula. The first misty wisps of the cosmic cloud began to curl around the ship as it rattled its way onwards at top speed.

"It's strange," he mused, "we're getting away from the *Revenge*, but my moustache is still quivering like a Canalopian banjo string."

"There's something about this I don't like," said Barney, twisting his tentacles with worry.

"Terrible bad luck," Pegg said blackly. Legg nodded sadly.

The gassy clouds of the nebula closed around the *Jolly Apollo*, hiding them completely from view.

Small rocks drifted by in the mist, with dark shapes moving on them.

Zlit let go of the wheel and staggered to the back of the ship. "I don't like it, Cap'n," he cried.

"Oh no, it can't be," said Vulpus, peering at the passing rocks. "It is! Look – *crabs*."

Stranded!

He pointed at a large rock which was covered with scuttling crustaceans.

"Crabs on the rock, you're in for a shock," recited Pegg, with terror etched on his face.

"What's wrong with a few crabs?" Sam asked the cowering crew.

But most of them were superstitiously tying themselves in knots, trying to tap their elbows with their knees, or reciting the pirate code backwards to ward off trouble.

Sam looked at the jabbering pirates and sighed. *Well, we've got to do something,* he thought to himself, grabbing the wheel to steer the *Jolly Apollo* deeper into the nebula. "If we go in here then Black-Hole *Weird* won't be able to find us – and if he can't find us then he can't pinch the map, or the grum," Sam explained.

He turned to look at the crew – but the pirates still looked *petrified*.

Sam looked at the scared pirates and felt a tremor of dread.

All around the ship the mists of the dark nebula swirled, and shadows on the rocks scratched and

scuttled. "What's *wrong*?" he asked.

"It's this place!" shouted Captain Comet. "Don't you know where you've brought us?"

"No," said Sam, a heavy feeling settling in his stomach.

"It's the Crab Nebula!" hissed Comet.

The very mention of the name set the crew weeping and wailing.

"The Crab Nebula?" Sam replied. "That doesn't sound so bad."

"*Really*?" said Comet sarcastically. "No ship that enters the Crab Nebula ever returns!"

Chapter Four
TRAPPED

Stranded!

The thick gas clouds of the nebula surrounded the *Jolly Apollo*. Half of the crew had broken open a barrel of grum and the other half were frantically packing. The three that could write were scribbling letters home.

"Oh, woe is us!" moaned Barney.

"Cursed to suffer the horrors of the Crab Nebula!" cried another.

"Yeah, nice work, small fry," snarled Pegg.

The crew stared at Sam accusingly.

"I didn't know it was the Crab Nebula!" Sam protested. "And we had to get away from Black-Hole Beard. We couldn't let him get the map. My parents are counting on us."

"We can't help your parents if we're crab-food," said Legg sadly.

"You know what they say about the Crab Nebula?" said Pegg crossly.

"Well no, actually," said Sam with a sigh.

"*Those who in the crab cloud do sail,*

Will weep and cry and shout and wail," replied Zlit. "And that's just *one* of the sayings!"

31

"And they say there's a monstrous race that live here," Romero gulped.

"They eat pirates for breakfast," Zlit said, snapping his jaws.

"And lunch!" Barney said, wobbling his tentacles around nervously.

"No, listen to me!" said Sam. "It's OK! We can just turn around and go back. We haven't travelled very far into the nebula so it'll be easy to navigate our way out. And if this place is so scary then Black-Hole Beard won't risk trying to find us. Even if he does we're so well hidden it would be easier to find a Paloobian Jink Flea in a Strumian Hair Beast."

"Hey – my mother was a Strumian Hair Beast!" said Strax.

"But to be fair," said Pegg, "she did have fleas."

"And they *were* hard to find," added Legg.

"All we have to do is wait here until we think Black-Hole Beard has got bored, then we can continue on our way," Sam reasoned.

There was a minute of silence, and then

the pirates cheered in relief. Suddenly everyone was clinking their grum glasses happily and unpacking their bowling shoes.

"Well, in that case," said Comet, the swagger returning to his demeanour, "why don't we have that game of bowling I was talking about? And I'll put up this as a prize to the winner."

He held up his golden fob watch – a fine timepiece that could tell the precise hour in three different galaxies at the same time.

A huge cheer went up from the crew.

"Hurray for Comet!" they cried. "The best captain under the seven suns!"

Sam raised his eyes to the heavens as the distracted crew clattered happily below decks. Then he spotted the Kraken, Barney, standing by the ship's rails with his tentacles dangling over the side.

"Not coming, Barney?" Sam asked.

"No," he replied, with an excited smile on his face. "Fresh crab is my favourite – I'm going fishing."

He took a series of crab nets from the storage place on the deck and started throwing them over the side of the ship. Sam smiled and left him to it. He knew that no matter how tasty the crabs were, Barney would ruin them with his cooking.

Below decks the bowling competition had already started. The *Jolly Apollo* may have been a terrible pirate ship, but it was an excellent place to go bowling. The wide hull of the spaceship meant that the *Apollo* could comfortably fit three bowling lanes into the space – instead of the normal one lane found on most pirate ships. Not only that, but in the space that other ships would use for laser cannons, the *Apollo*'s crew had squeezed in another two bowling lanes.

Sam grabbed a foaming glass of lemonady grum and wandered over to where Comet was preparing to bowl. Through a mixture of skill, rule-bending and outright cheating, Captain Comet was the *Apollo*'s bowling champion, and it was not a title he was going to lose without a fight – whether it was a fair one or not. Last time Sam had played the captain, Comet had nudged the cabin boy just as he was about to bowl, coughed and sneezed to distract Sam, and had even taken extra goes, saying the first ones had just been "a practice".

But this match was between Comet and a Snippernaut called Romero. Unfortunately for Comet, none of his tricks were working against Romero. In the last round of bowling the scores were tied. The tension had clearly got to Comet. His first ball missed all ten pins.

35

"Blistering barnacles!" he wailed. "That ball is clearly broken!"

The crew laughed as Comet showed the ball around, pointing out a small mark on the surface.

"Use mine, Cap'n," offered Vulpus.

Comet took the new ball and readied himself. He took aim, swung his arm back and hurled the ball as hard as he could. It was a terrible shot that bounced twice and leapt right over the pins.

"Curse this slippery track!" he shouted. "Who's been over-polishing this lane?"

Sam grinned. The slipperiness of the lane hadn't been a problem when Comet was winning.

"Romero just needs one hover pin to win," commentated Legg.

"And he'll break Comet's bowling

record as well!" sniggered Pegg.

Romero sauntered confidently over to the lane, his lucky bowling ball held firmly in his lobster-like pincers. He slowly drew his arm back, ready to strike…

"Well! I think Black-Hole Beard is probably long gone now, so all hands on deck and let's get out of this nebula," said Comet, clapping his hands together.

The crew laughed and booed. Romero threw his bowling ball down and snapped his claws angrily.

"Yes, well, can't be helped," said Comet shamelessly. "Let's remember what we're meant to be doing – finding Planet X, not bowling! Romero, let's call it a draw. You had me worried there for a while, but to be honest I think the pressure was about to get to you. Actually, this probably saved you some embarrassment."

The crew trooped up on deck, joking about Comet's brazen cheek. They all agreed he was a massive cheat – but as pirates they quite admired that. They laughed as they readied the spaceship for its journey. But minutes later they still hadn't moved.

"Cap'n, I think you should see this!" called Legg.

The two-headed first mate was standing next to the instrument panel by the ship's wheel.

"Everything's gone haywire, Cap'n," he explained as Comet and the rest of the crew gathered around. "It must be this here nebula – the instruments are all pointing in different directions."

"What does that mean?" asked Sam.

"What it means, shipmate," replied Comet, looking worried, "is that we're flying blind. So I don't know how we're going to find our way out!"

38

Chapter Five
SPACE TRAWLER

If there was one thing that the crew of the *Jolly Apollo* was used to, it was getting lost. However, this time it was different. Normally there were stars and planets around and eventually someone in the crew would recognize one of them and they would find their way again. It usually took a long time, but they would do it. Surrounded by the thick dust clouds of the Crab Nebula, the crew could see nothing but the occasional crab-covered lump of rock. It didn't look good.

Sam grabbed one of the telescopes, hoping against hope that the extra power would help him see something through the fog.

"I've got as much chance of seeing something if I put the telescope to one of these," said Comet, tapping one of his eye patches.

"So much for your great idea," Pegg grumbled bitterly.

Sam felt terrible. *Pegg's right,* he thought. *It was my idea to come here.*

"Leave the kid alone," said Barney. "He's saved us before and he'll do it again."

Sam didn't feel so sure, but he appreciated the vote of confidence.

"And why are you so cheery, Tentacle Toes?" said Pegg.

"Well, one, I trust Sam. And two, I've got these," Barney replied, holding up a net full of crabs. "I've only ever seen these at the fish market at Piscus 5. You can only harvest them in this nebula."

"You can buy them?" asked Sam excitedly.

"Sure, but they're very expensive…"

"But if you can buy them, then ships *do* get out of here!" cried Sam triumphantly. "All we have to do is find a space trawler and follow it."

"Oh, is that all?" said Pegg sarcastically.

"Do you have a better idea?" asked Legg. "No, I thought not."

"Pegg and Legg are arguing again, so that might be a good sign," said Comet doubtfully. "But how we're going to spot anything in this cloud is beyond me."

"We don't have to see a trawler," said Barney.

41

"We can smell one. These crabs taste great, but they really stink something awful once they've been caught. We'll smell a ship full of them from way off."

He thrust his catch at the crew, who wrinkled their noses at the stench.

"Come on then," said Sam. "Let's get sniffing!"

Nearly a day had passed before the unmistakable waft of caught-crab hit the *Jolly Apollo*. Slowly the pirates guided the ship towards the smell. A shape became visible through the mist – the outline of a space trawler. But something wasn't right – the ship was leaning over on one side and it looked like it was limping rather than flying.

As the *Apollo* got closer they could see why –
one side of the trawler's hull had been torn open.
A huge pincer-shaped hole gaped in the side of
the ship.

"Aye, aye, what's this then?" asked Comet.

"Looks like we *both* need help," said Sam.

"Bring the *Apollo* alongside, we're going to
investigate," commanded Comet.

The pirate ship moored next to the trawler and dropped its gravity anchor. Sam went across with some of the crew. The fishermen looked petrified, cowering on the decks as the pirates stepped aboard.

"Do not fear, it's Captain Joseph Hercules Invictus Comet to the rescue!" Comet announced grandly, stabbing his laser cutlass in the air at every word.

"Errr, maybe put the laser cutlass down?" Sam suggested, as the fishermen shrank back further in fear.

Comet slipped the cutlass in his belt and bowed deeply. "I assure you that under the oath of the pirate code, I am here to help. Yes, I may be the galaxy-famous buccaneer but I mean you no harm. Perhaps you may have heard of me?"

Comet looked at them expectantly. The crew of the trawler looked blank.

"Captain Comet… fearless leader of the blood-thirsty crew of the *Jolly Apollo*…?" said Comet hopefully, waving an arm in the general direction

of his ship. The crew looked bored and thirsty rather than fearsome and threatening.

The fisherman looked none the wiser until one of them stepped forwards with a wide smile on his face.

"Ahhh, Captain Comeet!"

The trawlerman nudged his fellow crewmen. He tucked his hands under his armpits and waggled his arms like wings, clucking louder than a Pangolian chicken.

"Comeet, Comeet!" he cried. "Cluck, cluck, cluuuuuck, cluck."

Suddenly the rest of the fishermen knew exactly who Comet was and they erupted into laughter.

"Boo!" shouted one of the fishermen. The one who was being a chicken then pretended to wet his pants – much to the amusement of the others.

"How odd," said Comet. "It must be a local dance or something – perhaps one of gratitude?"

The crew of the *Jolly Apollo* smirked knowingly.

"Anyhow, we haven't got time for this!" Comet raised his voice to a shout and started gesticulating wildly. "TELL MEEE, my GOOD FEL-LOWS. What HAP-pen-ed to your VES-sel?"

The trawlermen looked blankly at Comet.

"Perhaps I can help, Captain?" said Barney.

"Now, Barney, much as I appreciate your kind offer I really can't see what your, errm, *unique* cooking skills will add to this particular situation."

But Barney was already chatting to the trawlermen in a language that sounded to Sam like a sequence of burps and slurps.

"Barney, you can speak their language!" he exclaimed.

Barney blushed slightly. "Yes, I found that if you want the best crabs you've got to be able to talk to the fishermen. Picked up that tip years ago. Ooh, I got some delicious crabs back then – cooked them in a sauce made of—"

"Yes, yes, I'm sure it was lovely," said Comet irritably, "but what caused the damage to their ship?"

"I forgot to ask," said Barney. He spoke to

them again.

The fishermen all started talking at once.

"Ooooh," said Barney in reply. "Oh dear."

"So?" asked Comet.

"Well, apparently," said Barney, "it was like a crab, but one as big as an asteroid with claws twice as big as the *Apollo*!"

Suddenly Comet looked pale. "I wish I hadn't asked," he said.

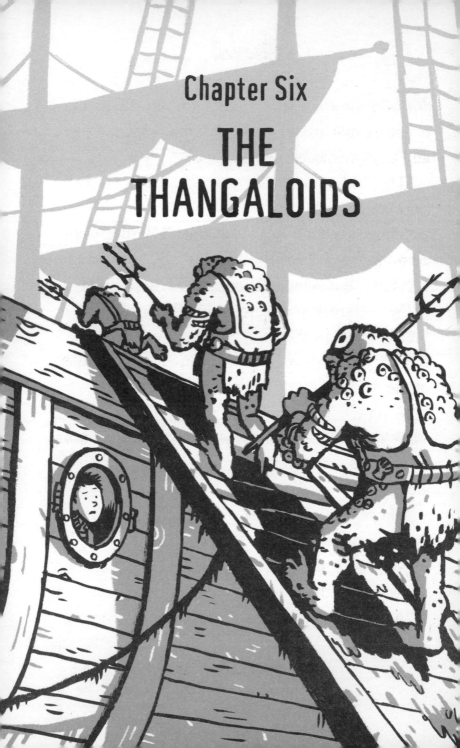

Chapter Six

THE THANGALOIDS

Stranded!

While the trawlermen filled Barney in on the exact details of the monster-crab attack, Pegg and Legg inspected the damage.

"This old stink tub is in no condition to fly," said Pegg sourly.

"They asked if we can tow them," Barney said, coming over.

"Out of the nebula?" Legg asked, hopefully.

"No," Barney shook his head. "They went a bit funny when I asked if they knew the way out. But they said there's a small port in the middle of the nebula."

"A port?" Sam said in surprise. "That's great! They'll be able to tell us the way out. See, not everyone's as scared of this nebula as you lot are."

"Those fishermen look pretty scared to me…" Pegg snorted.

"We don't have much choice," Comet sighed. "Barney, tell them we'll tow them to the port."

"A port full of pirate-eating monsters..." Barney whispered.

As the port appeared through the mists, Sam felt more and more nervous. He tried to keep calm in front of the crew, but he was worried they were heading into danger. As they got closer to the big asteroid the port was built on, his stomach lurched like he'd just had second helpings of one of Barney's dinners.

The *Jolly Apollo* docked and lowered its gangplank and the trawler moored alongside. The port didn't look dangerous – it seemed like a glorified fish market. Even from the deck Sam could see types and shapes of fish that he had never seen before.

"I think it's OK," he called to the crew, who were hiding below deck. "Barney, look at all these fish!"

Barney slid up to Sam and squealed. "Look at them, just look at them! There's grungfish, and

a hoopla eel – you can't find them anywhere these days!"

Barney took an excited step on to the gangplank – and three huge blue aliens stepped on to the other end and started marching towards them. They were tall and burly, with slimy suckers sprouting all over their bald heads and faces.

"I don't like the look of this…" Sam muttered as he and Barney hurried back up the gangplank on to the *Jolly Apollo*. The rest of the crew were there, looking decidedly nervous. Sam looked over to the trawler – where more blue aliens were leading the captain away.

"Who are they?" Sam asked Captain Comet.

Comet was trembling so much his eye patches were flapping.

"They're Thangaloids," Comet replied. "Quite possibly the meanest, grumpiest people in the

galaxy. The first thing you learn as a young deck-swabber is to stay well clear of Thangaloids. This is very, very bad news."

Sam groaned. "Do they really eat pirates?"

"No, but they don't like us," Comet shuddered. "They're the only people in the galaxy that don't like grum. They probably live here so they don't have to meet anyone, and we've just wandered up to their house and rung the doorbell."

"Nice," said Sam.

"There's no such word as 'nice' in the Thangaloid vocabulary. And there's no Thangaloid word for 'joke'. They replaced their sense of humour with a sense of violence."

"Silence!" shouted the lead Thangaloid in a voice that sounded like a bucket of broken glass being stirred with a mallet. "Who is captain of this…" he looked sneeringly around the *Apollo*, "…vessel?"

"He is," said Comet, pointing at Sam.

The Thangaloid peered suspiciously at them both.

52

"So why," he asked, his face so close to Comet's that the luckless pirate could see the Thangaloid's slime-filled suckers, "do you have a badge with 'I'm the Captain' written on it?"

"Oh, erm, that, it's, erm… a birthday treat?" Comet replied.

"Take this snivelling coward away," the Thangaloid ordered.

One of the other Thangaloids grabbed Comet's coat collar.

"Easy there, me hearty," protested Comet as he was dragged away. "That's Galvonian velvet, it creases terribly. It'll be awfully difficult to get the slime out…" Comet's voice faded away as the Thangaloid hauled him down the gangplank. The other Thangaloid glared at the *Apollo*'s crew.

"As for the rest of you, follow me. Don't even think about trying anything – though I doubt you'd have the nerve."

The crew of the *Apollo* trooped down the gangplank and joined the trawlermen as they were marched behind their captain. They were herded to the other side of the dock where Comet and the trawler captain were thrown to their knees in front of a huge throne made entirely from crab shells. Sat on the throne was a gigantic, Thangaloid. His skin was slimier than the others Sam had seen and was covered in even more suckers. The other Thangaloids all bowed as they approached him, so Sam guessed that this must be the king.

"So," said the king, his deep voice thick with menace, "how much crab have you brought back today?"

The fisherman began to frantically burp and slurp a reply. Barney leaned over to Sam and started to translate.

"He's saying they were attacked by a monster…"

"Silence, worm!" the king interrupted the fisherman. "I do not want to hear your life story! I want to see how many crabs you have caught! Weigh the catch!"

Two Thangaloids carried over a large net

containing the same type of crabs Barney had been catching earlier.

The net was dumped on to a gigantic set of scales. Sam watched nervously as the dial moved, as did the snivelling trawler captain. When the dial stopped, he let out a cry and threw himself at the king's feet.

Barney leaned over to Sam. "He's pleading for mercy," the Kraken said.

The Thangaloid king leaned so far over the trawler captain that some slime from his forehead dripped on to the unfortunate fisherman.

"Pathetic!" the king barked. "Guards, take this fool away and throw him into the black hole!"

The trawler captain was dragged to his feet and carried away, howling and sobbing and burping pathetically.

"You!" barked the king, pointing at one of the trawlermen. "You are the new captain. Do not fail me!"

The trawlermen were chased away back to their ship. The king's evil eyes alighted on Captain Comet.

"And you?" he said.

"Ah, yes, ahem," said Comet. "There's obviously been some terrible mistake here. You see, we're not fishermen, we just got lost. Now if you could just give us directions for how to get out of this nebula then we'll leave right away. As far as we're concerned we don't even know you're here." Comet tapped the side of his nose conspiratorially.

"Yes, there has been a mistake, you snivelling space maggot," the king replied, pulling himself up to his huge blubbery height. "You haven't brought me any crabs."

"Oh right," said Comet, cowering under the king's gaze. "I'm sure that can be arranged, can't it me hearties?" He appealed to the Apollo's crew. "And how many would you like? Enough for a light snack? A handful? Perhaps a sack?"

The king bellowed with irritation. "No one may

57

leave my nebula until they bring me the weight of their ship – in crabs!"

"But that would be," said Comet to himself, "now let's see, twenty-five times seven... no, twenty-seven... no, no, I've forgotten the anchor, so add four and carry three, erm... two hundred, no, two thousand, no, no it's... That's a lot of crabs!" He mopped his brow with a brightly coloured handkerchief. "But if we bring them to you, then we can go free?" he asked meekly.

"Of course," the king replied. His big, blue, bulbous body began to jiggle and his suckers started to shake. Sam realised that the king was laughing – it was not a pretty sight. "But don't count your crabs before you've caught them," the king chortled. "No one yet has ever brought me enough. And if you fail, the only journey you will be going on is to the centre of the black hole! Mwa ha ha! Mwa ha ha!"

Comet's right, Sam thought miserably. *Thangaloids have no sense of humour.* Things were looking bleak for the crew of the *Jolly*

Apollo, but they were about to get a whole lot worse. Another laugh joined in with that of the Thangaloid king – and this one was horribly familiar.

"It can't be," said Sam.

But it was. As Sam and the crew watched in horror, the tall figure of Black-Hole Beard appeared from behind the throne.

Chapter Seven
TAX TIME

Stranded!

A malicious smile split Black-Hole Beard's face like a sword wound and his yellowing teeth looked like crooked tombstones.

"Well said, Your Majesty," Black-Hole Beard laughed.

"Black-Hole Beard?" said Comet.

"Observant as ever, Comet," taunted the evil pirate.

"But… but…" stammered Comet.

"And as eloquent as ever, too," the evil pirate mocked. "Let me explain before your tiny brain explodes. I came looking for you and ended up here. Unluckily for you, Slebus here and I are old friends." Black-Hole Beard slapped the Thangaloid king on the back, making a wet squelching sound. "In fact, he used to be on my crew before he became king. Those were the days, eh, Slebby?" Black-Hole Beard gave a roaring laugh. The Thangaloid king didn't even smile.

"So if you'll give me the map, and you tell me how to get out of here," Black-Hole Beard nodded towards the Thangaloid king, "I'll be on my way."

"That's not fair!" Comet bleated.

"Cork your blow-hole, Comet!" barked Black-Hole Beard. "Not fair? You sound like a baby blubber worm – you're an embarrassment to pirates everywhere."

But the Thangaloid king was stroking his suckers thoughtfully. "True. *All* ships must pay the tax. I'm afraid you too must bring me the weight of *Gravity's Revenge* in crab, my old friend."

"What?" Black-Hole Beard yelled furiously.

The Thangaloid king stood up and his guards stepped closer, suckers bristling angrily.

The mean pirate stepped back and controlled himself. "Fine," he said, through gritted teeth. "I'll get you yer crab. But then you give me the map, and the directions."

"Of course," the Thangaloid king said with a steely glint in his eyes. "But crabs first. You will set sail tomorrow and have until the third chiming of the port bell to return." The Thangaloid king waved them away. "Succeed and go free. Fail and die."

Comet bowed to the king and turned to his crew. He was white as a sheet as he twisted his hat in his hands. Black-Hole Beard stormed past him.

"Ha! It's not going to be as easy as you thought, Black-Hole Beard. Hope you like fishing!" Sam called after him.

Black-Hole Beard turned to him, his face twisted in an angry snarl. "I'll get that map from you, you'll see," he spat. "After all, Comet won't need it when he's being sucked down a black hole."

The crew bustled about the *Jolly Apollo*, readying it for the fishing trip, sorting out nets, buckets and anything else that could be used for catching crabs. Looking up from his work, Sam realised that the mists inside the nebula had thinned slightly. He nudged Pegg and Legg to let them know.

"Excellent," said Legg. "That'll make looking for them crabs a bit easier."

"But it also means we get more of an eyeful of that," grumbled Pegg.

He pointed over to where *Gravity's Revenge* was moored. It towered over the *Apollo* and every other ship in the dock like a thundercloud before a storm. They seemed to be taking things surprisingly easy – apart from taunting the *Apollo*, that is. The *Revenge*'s crew hurled insults as they leaned over the rails of their ship.

"Look, a boat full of crab food! That'll be handy."

"Who's your next captain going to be when

Comet gets chucked down the hole?"

"Call that a knot, you useless sea slug? Me granny can tie better knots than that and she's only got feet!"

"How come they're not doing anything?" asked Vulpus, the red-furred *Apollo* crewmate.

"They must be up to something," said Sam.

"They're *always* up to something," said Pegg.

"Yes, but what is it this time?" Sam wondered.

Even Black-Hole Beard got in on the act by shouting insults.

"Must be nice for you to see what a *real* pirate crew looks like, Comet," he taunted.

Comet and the rest of the crew burned with anger and humiliation. Pegg's face was bright red and Sam could hear the sound of his teeth grinding from across the deck.

"Just ignore them," said Sam. He shouted up at the *Revenge*. "Hey, if you're so great how come we've got a map to Planet X and you haven't?"

"Not for long, you insolent shrimp," Black-Hole Beard replied.

"We'll see about that," said Sam to the *Apollo*'s crew. "Look, we've got loads in our favour. *Gravity's Revenge* is much heavier than the *Apollo* so they'll have to catch more crabs. Secondly, we've got Barney." Sam dropped his voice a little. "He may be a useless cook, but," he raised his voice again, "he's a top class fisherman – aren't you, Barney?"

"Mmm-mm," Barney agreed, his mouth stuffed full of crab that he'd caught earlier.

"By the craters of Zooton!" shouted Pegg. "We'll never catch enough if that tentacled buffoon keeps eating them!"

Stranded!

The port bell rang, signalling the start of the day. Each ship had to be weighed first on a giant set of space scales by the side of the port. The trawler went first, their new captain looking even more nervous than Captain Comet.

Gravity's Revenge was next. But before the ship moved on to the scales, it hovered in mid-space for a while. Suddenly boxes, barrels and sea chests were hurled over the side, followed swiftly by a number of crew members, too.

"What's going on?" Sam asked.

"It's Black-Hole Beard – he's making his ship lighter," said Piole.

"That's terrible," said Sam, aghast at Black-Hole Beard's ruthlessness.

"That's cheating!" said Legg.

"I could think of some useless weight I'd like to chuck overboard," said Pegg, giving Barney an evil glare.

Once *Gravity's Revenge* had flown away from the scales, it was the *Jolly Apollo*'s turn.

Sam watched in horror as the

number showing their weight crept higher and higher.

"Erm, OK," Sam gulped as they got their final reading. "Who'd have thought this old ship would weigh that much. But never mind, eh, Captain? Captain?"

The crew looked to Captain Comet for some stirring words, a small speech to inspire them, to encourage them to strive their hardest, to tackle the insurmountable odds, to fight the good fight. But Comet was staring at the scales with a frantic look on his face.

"We're doomed," Comet yelled. "DOOMED!"

Chapter Eight
MONSTER CRAB

The crew of the *Apollo* were used to hearing Captain Comet predict their imminent demise, but this time he seemed to have a point.

"How do we even find crabs?" asked Romero gloomily.

"Oh, that's easy," Barney replied. He was by far the happiest member of the crew – a whole day's crab fishing was his idea of heaven. "The crabs live in burrows on the rocks and asteroids. All we need to do is look for rocks."

"See, Captain, it's quite straightforward, really," said Sam, trying to spread the positive mood. Comet sat hunched up in the middle of the deck with his hat pulled down low and arms around his knees."That's easy for you to say, you're not the one looking down the wrong end of a black hole," he grumbled.

"But, Captain, the crew needs you," Sam replied.

"OK, OK," Comet muttered. "All hands on deck; eyes peeled for rocks."

After drifting aimlessly around for a while there

was a shout from the crow's nest.

"Rocks ahoy – starboard side!"

The crew rushed to the side rails of the *Apollo*. Even though the rocks were shrouded in mist they could still see hundreds of crabs scuttling all over them. Comet visibly brightened at the sight.

"Get those nets ready, my boys – we're going fishing!"

The *Apollo* drew up alongside the rocks and dropped the gravity anchor. There were thousands of crabs scuttling around on their little orange legs and popping up from their burrows.

"Now the key to successful crab fishing," Barney whispered, "is to be very quiet and don't make any sudden movements. Softly, softly, catchy crabby."

The crew started to tip-toe around and readied their nets to cast them over the rails to catch the crabs. Every little noise brought a chorus of "Shhh!".

KABOOM!

PARP PARP PARP!

WHOOO-WEEE WHOOO-WEEE!

Gravity's Revenge broke from the mist with its horns and klaxons blaring and laser cannons firing. The sudden noise startled everyone, including the crabs, which scuttled for cover down their burrow holes in the rocks.

"Oh, great!" spat Comet. "Now we'll have to wait for them to come out."

"No chance of that," Barney replied glumly. "Once they've been scared off they won't be back for the rest of the day."

"We'd better find somewhere new then," said Sam.

"Look at them, laughing at us," said Comet, as the *Revenge* pulled away.

"I don't understand," said Pegg. "Those scurvy dogs might be scaring away our crabs but they're not fishing for any either."

"So what are they up to?" said Legg.

"Look – that's what!" said Sam.

He pointed ahead to where the *Revenge* had pulled up alongside a trawler. Black-Hole Beard and his crew were menacing the fisherman with laser cutlasses and muskets and forcing them to hand over their catch.

"That's totally against the pirate code!" said Comet indignantly.

"I thought pirates were meant to pinch stuff," asked Sam.

"Not *fish*," said Comet. "Treasure, jewels, all that stuff. But fish? No, no, no. That's just depriving a working man of his livelihood."

"Even if it is against the code, it's working," said Sam. "We'd better find a new place to go fishing or we're going to lose the map."

"And more importantly – you'll lose a captain!" cried Comet.

The good news for Comet was that they found another excellent fishing spot very quickly. There was no sign of *Gravity's Revenge* either. The crew got their nets out and after a short while a large haul of crabs began to appear on deck. Comet leaned nonchalantly on the rails, watching the mountain of crab grow ever higher.

"Hah, me hearties, that's the ticket! We'll have this old ship stuffed to the gunwales!" he crowed. "All we need do is stay away from Black-Hole Beard."

No sooner had Comet spoken than a large, dark shadow could be seen in the mist ahead of them.

"Oh you've *got* to be joking!" said Comet, slapping a hand to his head. "It's *Gravity's Revenge*! OK boys, try to hide as many of these crabs as you can before Black-Hole Beard pinches them."

"It's moving in a very strange way," said Romero.

"He's right, Captain," Legg confirmed. "It

seems to be going sideways."

"Sideways? What manner of problem makes a ship travel sideways?" asked Comet.

Sam looked at the crabs scuttling around on deck, then at the huge shape looming out of the mist.

"Errr, I don't think it's the *Revenge*," Sam gulped.

"Good, good," said Comet.

"Actually, I don't think it's going to be very good either," Sam said, pointing up at the great shape in horror. "Look!"

The mists slowly parted and the crew of the *Apollo* saw exactly what it was.

"The monster crab!" Comet gasped.

"Those trawlermen weren't kidding," said Sam, staring up in awe at the giant creature ahead of them. "It's HUGE! It must be ten times bigger than the ship!"

The crab picked its way across the space rocks on its eight legs – each one thicker than the *Apollo*'s main mast. Its eyes waved on two short, squat stalks on the top of its shell. As the crew watched in horror, a mouth like a giant hydraulic crusher opened to show a black hole more terrifying than the sucking vortex next to the port. Most terrible of all were its claws – each one twice the size of a spaceship and ridged with fearsome points.

The monster stopped and waved its claws, as if tasting space with its pincers.

"I don't think it's seen us," Sam breathed.

"Then let's get out of here," Comet whispered nervously. "Mr Piole, reverse thrust, if you please – gentle as she goes."

The *Apollo* moved slowly backwards and the

crab didn't react.

"It's working," said Comet.

"Softly, softly, hide from crabby," whispered Barney.

"No, look!" cried Sam.

Behind them, right in the direction the *Jolly Apollo* was going, sat *Gravity's Revenge*, blocking the way, its laser cannons bristling.

"Look out!" shout Legg. "It's going to shoot!"

KAWHOOSH!

The blast from the cannon streaked past the *Apollo*.

"He missed!" crowed Comet.

KABOOM!

The shot hit the crab full on the shell. The crab reared up angrily, snapping its pincers together.

"Uh-oh," said Comet.

The *Revenge* fired up its rocket boosters and streaked away, leaving the *Apollo* to face the wrath of the crab alone. The monster crab loomed over the pirate ship. It raised its pincers, ready to crush the spaceship in its terrible claws.

"Quick!" squeaked Comet. "Full speed reverse!"

Piole hit the thrust lever but rather than firing the *Apollo* to safety, the boosters spluttered, backfired and died.

"I really must get those engines serviced," mused Comet distractedly.

"Too late now, you great lummox," shouted Pegg.

With a sound of crunching metal, the monster crab grabbed hold of the *Jolly Apollo*'s mast. As the ship

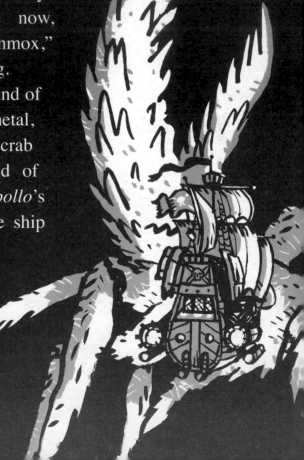

tilted, Sam grabbed hold of the rail. Comet grabbed hold of Sam.

"I'm too good-looking to die," he wailed.

The crab lifted the *Apollo* towards its terrible jaws. Its mouth was easily the size of three ships, the jagged edge of its mouth like a mountain range of doom.

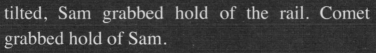

"And I'm *certainly* too good-looking to die in something that smells like that!" Comet added, as the stench of the crab's breath swept over the doomed ship.

With a sudden twitch of its pincer, the crab flicked the ship into its mouth and swallowed it whole.

Chapter Nine
KABOOM!

Sam felt his way across the pitch-black deck and found what he hoped was the right box. He had never experienced dark like this and he struggled not to panic. *Maybe this was how my parents felt when they crashed?* Shaking away the thought, he felt around inside the box until his fingers closed over what he prayed was the right tube. Taking it out, he pulled a tab and the emergency flare spluttered into life.

In the bright green glow of the flare Sam could see his fellow crewmates huddled in groups on the deck.

"Everyone OK?" he called.

There were muffled replies from around the ship.

"Where in the name of Starry Jones' locker are we?" asked Comet.

Sam held the flare as high as he could. The greenish light showed them to be in a large, cavern-like hole. The *Apollo* was floating in what looked like dirty water.

"Are we in a cave?" asked Barney.

"Of course we're not, you leggy nincompoop!" snapped Pegg.

"The crab's gobbled us up," explained Legg.

"I've been eaten by lunch!" wailed Barney.

"Do not fear, my boys," cried Comet. "I've been eaten many times by various animals: a striped Thangor on Ulan Mantor, a Jumblesnitch on Excrea 3, and even by a Grimbled Slime Toad in the Baloogan Marshes…"

The crew pulled a face at the last one.

"But I have always survived."

"How?" asked Barney.

"Generally the animal got terrible indigestion and died," said Comet.

"So your plan is to wait for the crab to get indigestion and die, then try to get out?" said Pegg.

"Erm, basically, yes," Comet replied.

"I don't think we've got time for that," said Sam. "Look."

He pointed down over the side of the ship. There was a hissing sound and the water next to the hull was bubbling.

"It looks like the water's melting the bottom of the ship," he explained.

"I don't think that's water," said Legg. "If we're inside a crab then that must be its stomach acid!"

"That makes sense," said Barney. "Crabs can eat anything, so their digestive juices must be really acidic."

"Do they get indigestion?" asked Comet hopefully.

"No, now you mention it, I don't think they do," Barney replied.

"Great! We don't even have the captain's useless plan to fall back on," grumbled Pegg. "All that's left is to wait here until we dissolve."

"We might not have to wait for that," said Legg brightly.

"Really?" asked Comet, hope flickering again.

"I think *they* might get us first," replied Legg, pointing upwards to where what looked like stalactites hung from the inside of the crab's stomach. "Those are its stomach teeth – they'll probably grind us before we dissolve."

"Oh well, that's that then," sighed Comet.

"No!" said Sam. "I haven't been with you lot for long, but already I've found the best friends I've ever had, and been on adventures I could only dream about before. Sure, you're useless pirates but who else can say that they've dodged grumigators and outwitted Black-Hole Beard? And we did that together, as a team. I'm not going to let that go without a fight. I owe that to my parents and we owe it to each other. Let's show this oversized crustacean who's boss!"

"Aye, aye!" cheered the crew.

Sam's flare went out.

"Oh," said the crew.

Sam fumbled for another flare and lit it.

"Aye, aye!" cheered the crew.

"So, do you have a plan?" whispered Comet.

"All I've got in my head is an old story my mum used to read me when I was younger," said Sam.

"Sam, I don't think this is the right time for a bedtime story," said Comet.

"Listen," said Sam, "it was about a man who was swallowed by a whale. He got free by lighting a fire inside

the whale's stomach. The smoke made
the whale cough him out, or something
like that. I thought if we set off the rocket
boosters it might do something similar."

"Just what I was thinking!" exclaimed Comet.
"Mr Piole, do you think we can get those boosters
working this time?"

"Aye, aye, sir," said Piole, setting the controls.

"Brace yourselves, me hearties," shouted
Comet. "We're firing our way out of here. No
crab stops Captain Joseph Hercules Invictus
Comet! Full engine power, Mr Piole!"

Whuh-whuh-whuh-whuh, went the *Apollo*'s
engines as they failed to start properly. *Whuh-
whuh-whuh*.

"Typical,"
Comet muttered.
"Why can't those
blas—"

SPACE PIRATES

WHOOOOOOOOOOOOSSSSSSHHHHHHH!

The engines roared into life, the noise deafening in the crab's echoing stomach. The crew fell to the deck, clutching their ears. It was loud, but there wasn't any smoke.

"I don't think it's working," Sam cried above the noise.

Comet laid a sympathetic hand on Sam's arm. "Don't worry, Sam – it was a nice try!"

Their only real plan had failed.

Suddenly, everything began to shake. The crab's stomach acid jumped up and down like a stormy sea, and the ship was thrown from side to side. Sam grabbed hold of the main mast as a great rumble echoed around the cavern.

"Hold on tight!" Comet yelled. "She's gonna blow!"

Chapter Ten

GONE FISHING!

When Sam opened his eyes he was amazed to discover that he was still alive and still aboard the *Jolly Apollo*. Not only that, the rest of the crew was still there, too. It seemed much brighter – then Sam realised that was because the crab had disappeared. He sat up and gave his head a rub. A shower of white lumps fell on to his lap. He picked a piece up and sniffed it. It smelled of crab. He touched a bit with the end of his tongue. It tasted of crab. It was crab.

"Well, it's not quite what I had in mind," said Comet, slapping Sam on the back and plonking himself on the deck next to him. He was flecked with bits of crab too. "But it was very effective. Though Neptune knows how I'm going to get the mess out of this coat. Galvonian velvet is extremely difficult to clean."

"What happened?" asked Sam.

"I'm a bit hazy on the details myself," Comet admitted. "One moment the rocket boosters were firing away, next there was a big explosion and then the crab was in tiny pieces. And big pieces."

Comet waved airily at the space around the *Apollo*, which was filled with bits of exploded crab. Sam stared in wonder at the lumps, some as big as he was. Somehow the giant crab shell had survived the explosion, and was bumping from asteroid to asteroid.

"Basically," Comet continued, "big bangy, bye bye crabby."

"Gas," said the pirate called Jonjarama. He was notorious on the *Apollo* as the pirate with the worst wind. You didn't want to be trapped in a small space with Jonjarama after he'd been eating beans.

"Pardon?" Sam asked.

"Gas," Jonjarama repeated. "I reckons the crab had bad gas. It was probably his guts reacting badly to trying to digest the *Apollo*. I reckons it gave him gas and when the boosters were going the flames lit the gas and he exploded." Jonjarama did his own bum explosion for emphasis.

"Wow!" said Sam.

"So basically, what you're saying is he got

chronic indigestion! Ha! See? My plan worked! He got indigestion and died and now we're free," said Comet proudly. He stood up and dusted himself down. "Right, me hearties, no need to thank me – we've got fishing to do. Now, did we manage to hide any of those crabs we caught?"

"Well, there's good news and bad news on that score, Cap'n," said Vulpus.

"And the good news is?" asked Comet.

"We managed to hide all the crabs we caught in the hold," Vulpus replied.

"Excellent! And the bad news?"

"The crab's stomach acid has rotted the bottom of the ship away and they've all fallen out."

So you're telling me we don't have any crabs left?" asked Comet.

"One," said Vulpus. "We have one left."

Burp!

Everyone turned to see Barney dabbing his mouth with a napkin.

"Sorry," said Barney.

"It's all right, Barney, it's just wind," said Comet.

"No, sorry I… err… ate the last crab," replied Barney.

"Great, just great," said Comet, slapping his hand to his head. "How much time do we have left?" He fished the pocket watch out of his jacket and frantically checked all three of the times. "Quake me cutlass! We're nearly out of time! There's no way we can catch enough crab!" He started to pace the deck in a panic.

"I'm going to be thrown down a black hole. I'll be stretched like a Boolian Drango Hound! It's the end of Joseph Hercules Invictus Comet – pirate captain, adventurer and man of the people.

Cast away forever, and all because of some measly crabs."

The crew tried to console him – all apart from Sam who was standing by the *Apollo*'s rail looking out into space.

"Hold on a minute," said Sam. "We have to get the weight of the ship in crabs, right?"

Barney nodded.

"But no one said it had to be whole crabs," Sam grinned, pointing at the bits of crab floating past.

A slow grin spread over Barney's face as he looked at the white chunks bobbing all around them. "You mean…"

Sam picked up a net and hooked a nearby piece of crab out of the sky. "Come on – let's go fishing!"

As the third bell sounded at the Thangaloid port, Captain Comet and Sam were already waiting on the dockside. *Gravity's Revenge* was berthed in the dock nearby. From the way crabs were piled high on the decks and falling from the gun ports,

Sam guessed that their tactic of stealing other ship's catches had worked.

Black-Hole Beard sauntered along the dock to Comet and Sam with a smug expression on his face. He looked around with exaggerated effort.

"I can't see the *Apollo* anywhere, Comet – don't tell me you've managed to lose your ship as well as the map," he mocked.

Before anyone could answer, the Thangaloid king was brought to the side of the dock, his throne carried by four even stickier sweating Thangaloid warriors.

"The appointed hour has arrived," the king bellowed. "I hope for your own sakes that you have been successful! The black hole is always hungry for those who displease me." The king wiped a fleck of spit from his blubbery lips and looked pleased with himself.

"Let the weighing begin!" he called.

Gravity's Revenge was first. Black-Hole Beard grinned broadly as his first mate, Yarr, piloted the *Revenge* on to the scales.

"Sorry, Joseph, I hope I didn't scare your crabs away," he laughed. "Did you manage to catch any?"

"Cawr, couldn't catch a cold, couldn't catch a cold," squawked Baggot.

Comet and Sam looked on speechlessly as the *Revenge* was weighed. Black-Hole Beard's ship tipped the scales at double the weight they were before. The *Revenge's* crew cheered.

"There you go, Slebby, me old shipmate." Black-Hole Beard went to clap the Thangaloid king on the back, then seemed to think better of it. "I've brought ye the crab, now you keep your side of the deal. Their map, your directions."

"Best wait until the weighing's over, don't you think?" replied Comet.

"You!" barked the Thangaloid king. "Do you have your ship?"

"Yes, Your Majesty," Comet replied. "It's moored behind that asteroid over there."

"Bring it to the scales!" ordered the king. "Let me see if your ship has enough crabs, or whether it needs a new captain."

"Of course, Your Majesty," Comet replied with a low bow. "If you would be so good, Sam, as to summon the *Apollo*, please."

Sam fired a flare high over the dock – the sign Pegg and Legg had been waiting for. They lifted anchor and slowly started to sail out from behind the asteroid.

"How many crabs did you get anyway, Comet? I bet you've got less than one hundred," Black-Hole Beard sneered.

"You're right," Comet replied. "In fact, we've

just got one."

"One?" Black-Hole Beard exploded. "By the suns of Steperton Seven, you're even more useless than I thought!"

"You think?" Comet replied confidently, looking up at the *Apollo*.

Stranded!

As it edged into view, it was clear it was carrying something heavy. Slowly the Apollo revealed its secret – the monster crab shell, piled high with bits of crab. The crew had fished all the chunks of crab out of the sky, and Barney had even sprinkled some parsley on top.

They reached the scales, which showed that the stuffed crab shell was more than twice the weight of the pirate ship. Comet smiled the smile of someone who had cheated certain death once again. Sam was just relieved that Black-Hole Beard wasn't going to take the map after all.

"Nice work, Sam!" said Legg, pushing a foamy tankard of grum into his hand.

"Yeah, I suppose that wasn't bad," agreed Pegg as enthusiastically as he could.

"Three cheers for Sam!" shouted Piole.

"No," said Sam. "Three cheers for the *Jolly Apollo*!"

The cheers rang out from the *Apollo* and the trawler.

Across the dock, Captain Black-Hole Beard tore at his beard in rage and stormed around the dock, kicking crates of fish and hurling barrels into space.

"By the infernal holes of Julius Five!" he bellowed. "I'll get you for this!"

Chapter Eleven

ESCAPE

Captain Comet swaggered over to the Thangaloid king. He whipped the hat from his head and bowed extravagantly.

"Your Majesty," said Comet, "we have satisfied your terms and brought you your crab. I trust we are free to go?"

"You can't just let them leave!" Black-Hole Beard stormed. "We had a deal! Ye were on my crew!"

The Thangaloid king laughed. "And I learnt a lot from you, Blacky. Including the fact that deals can be renegotiated – especially if you no longer like the terms."

"What?" the evil pirate exploded. "You double-crossing, sucker-faced slime ball! No one cheats Black-Hole Beard and gets away with it!"

"Guards, take him away." The Thangaloid waved his hand lazily. "This Black-Hole Beard is for the black hole."

Two burly Thangaloid guards grabbed the *Gravity*'s captain and hauled him away.

"And as for you..." the Thangaloid king said,

102

turning to Comet with a steely stare.

"Your Majesty," said Sam, stepping forwards. "If I may humbly offer you some advice. Do you know who you are addressing? This is the captain who defeated the great crab monster of the nebula – turned a demon into dinner – a captain known across the galaxies for his daring and prowess."

This was all the introduction Captain Comet needed. If he was talented at anything, it was exaggerating.

"Indeed, I have battled with gas giants, wrestled with Gimbal gnomes and fought the Five Furies of Floximia Minor! So do not talk to me about

renegotiating deals or I'll show you what Captain Joseph Hercules Invictus Comet does when he is angry."

He pointed at the giant crab shell for emphasis.

"You speak well, Captain Comet," the king said, wiping the slime from his head thoughtfully. "And Thangaloids like a man who has proved himself. You are free to go. Come to me and I shall reveal the secret of how to escape the nebula."

Comet stepped up to the throne and the king leaned down and whispered into his ear.

"You mean, that's it?" said Comet. "That's how you get out?"

"It's simple but effective," shrugged the king.

"And could you tell us the way to the Corkscrew Galaxy? It's where we're headed next," said Sam.

"Don't push your luck," snapped the king, "or we'll see how true those tall tales of yours actually are." He turned to his guards. "Escort them back to their ship."

"Shouldn't we do something about Black-Hole

Beard?" Sam whispered to Comet. "I mean, isn't it the pirate code or something?"

"Yes it is," Comet replied, "but I reckon that the Thangaloids are more likely to end up in that hole rather than Black-Hole Beard. Now come on, we'd better haul anchor ourselves before the king changes his mind about us leaving port."

Comet and his crew headed back to the *Apollo* as quickly as decency would allow. Without further ado they cast off and sailed away from the Thangaloid dock.

"Mr Piole, set a course for first left at every asteroid we come to," said Comet.

The ship was soon out of the treacherous Crab Nebula. Sam and Comet stood on deck, looking at the vastness of space.

"Well, we escaped that one, but how do we get to the Corkscrew Galaxy?" said Comet, holding the scrap of map. "The galaxy is on the map, but the Crab Nebula isn't, so how do we know which direction to travel in?"

Suddenly Sam noticed a light behind them.

"Look Captain, we're being followed!" he said.

"What?" squawked Comet in a panic, fumbling for a telescope. "Is it the Thangaloids? Is it Black-Hole Beard?"

"No, it's the trawler we helped before," said Sam, "and they're flashing lights at us."

Comet peered through his telescope.

"Aha, it's Bortz Code," said Comet,

"the interstellar language of space travellers. Each flash means something different. Every pirate worth his spacesalt knows Bortz Code. Now what are they saying? 'Custard for the rose bush. Toothbrush in a bucket. Wash your pants on a Tuesday.' What in the name of Nibbles and his Jumblers are they on about?"

"Captain, a message from the trawler," shouted Vulpus from the crow's nest. "They're thanking us for helping them and for showing them the way out of the nebula. Also they say if we sail directly on from the twin stars dead ahead, we'll find the Corkscrew Galaxy."

"Of course," said Comet, snapping his telescope closed. "Just what I was saying. Signal back to thank them and ask if they're joining us."

Lights flashed between the two spaceships.

"Negative, Captain," Vulpus shouted down eventually. "They say the crabs from the nebula are too good to miss. Besides – now they know the way out they're not scared of the Thangaloids any more."

"Well, wish them the best of luck, Mr Vulpus, and we'll bid them farewell," Comet replied.

Just then the on-deck holoscreen flashed into life. Black-Hole Beard's angry face appeared on it. Behind him, the Thangaloid king was tightly bound and hanging over the black hole. He did not look best pleased.

"Comet, ye scurvy dog!" barked Black-Hole Beard. "Me and the king have had a little parley and we've agreed that I can go. He's been very obliging and told me where you're headed. I'm coming to get ye, Comet! And when I do…"

The image disappeared as Comet switched off the holoscreen.

"Goes on a bit, doesn't he?" said Comet. "Sam, ask Mr Piole to set a course for the Corkscrew Galaxy. Let's find that Planet X."

"And my parents!" Sam added. "Aye, aye, Cap'n Comet. Aye, aye!"

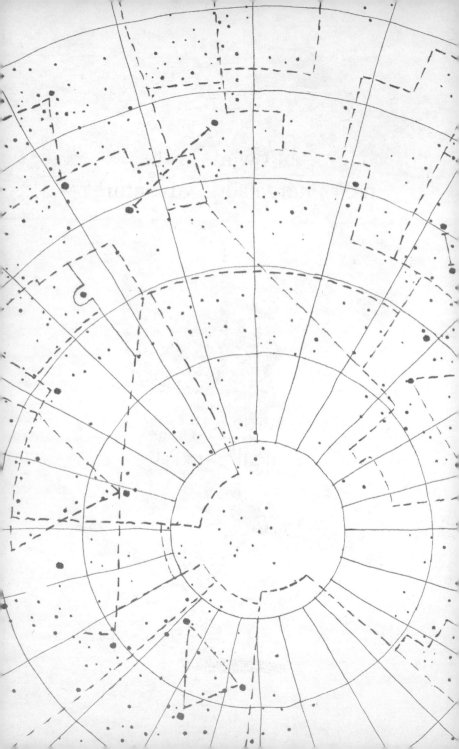

Can't wait for the
next intergalactic adventure?

Turn the page for
a sneaky peek!

Chapter One

CASTAWAY AHOY!

Samson Starbuck peered at the bowl of food in front of him and wrinkled his nose. Breakfast on board the pirate spaceship *Jolly Apollo* was never good, but today's looked *awful*. The bowl contained a thick grey liquid halfway between porridge and soup, which seemed to be both watery *and* lumpy at the same time. It smelled of old fish and engine oil.

As Sam stared at the bowl he was sure that something in it moved. Feeling sick, Sam pushed the bowl away from him and sat up. All around him in the mess hall, his fellow crew mates were digging into the disgusting gloop hungrily.

"How can you eat that?" Sam asked Piole, the pirate sitting next to him. "It's revolting!"

Piole turned to look at Sam, food dribbling from three of his twelve mouths.

"The food here is *always* revolting," Piole replied. "But it's the only food we get so you may as well make the most of it. Aren't you eating yours?"

"No, do you want it?" Sam knew the answer

already – Piole would eat just about anything.

"Cheers, me hearty!" said Piole, swapping Sam's bowl for his own empty one.

Sam felt the slap of a large tentacle on his shoulder and turned to see Barney, the ship's cook, standing behind him. Although Barney looked fearsome – he was a gigantic, multi-tentacled Kraken – he was actually Sam's best friend.

"Morning, Sam," said Barney. "Finished already? You must be growing – here, have some more!"

He slopped out another ladleful of the disgusting gloop into the empty bowl before wandering off, whistling a merry space shanty to himself. Sam groaned and leaned his head on the table.

"Growing?" Romero, the huge lobster-clawed snippernaut, guffawed. "Sam could grow for a Traxonion year and he'd still be a space sprat!"

"Hey!" Sam protested as the other pirates laughed.

"Aye, aye, shipmate," said Captain Comet, plonking himself down on the bench next to Sam.

Comet was one of the most extravagantly dressed space pirates in the Universe. He liked bright frock coats and always wore a tri-corn hat. He had eye patches covering two of his three eyes and a long waxed moustache that stuck out from each side of his face like curled wire.

Comet might look like a perfect pirate, but Sam knew he and his crew were widely regarded as the most useless space pirates in all the known galaxies – and probably the unknown galaxies as well. However, beneath all the bluster, bragging, incompetence and cowardice, Captain Comet had a heart of gold and truly cared for his crew.

Which was just as well, because Sam had joined the *Jolly Apollo* to try and rescue his parents, who had been space-shipwrecked on the mysterious Planet X. The pirates were only too happy to help. The planet was rumoured to be made of solid gold. And Sam had a map of how to get there!

"What's wrong, are you space-sick?" asked Captain Comet.

Sam shook his head.

"So what is it, me hearty? It can't be that bad!"

Sam picked up his bowl. The grey sludge shuddered and a bubble popped at the surface, releasing a smell like the inside of a bowling shoe.

"Oh," said Comet. "It *is* that bad." Comet grimaced and pushed the bowl towards Piole, who gave the captain a cheery wink.

"Anyhow," Comet continued, "I thought you'd like a quick status update – we're making good progress. We've passed the Corkscrew Galaxy and I think we should reach this wormhole soon." He pointed to the scrap of spacesuit material on which Sam's mother had drawn the map.

Sam raised his head and looked at it excitedly. They were getting closer by the minute! And they had managed not to get lost for three days now – a *Jolly Apollo* record.

"Castaway ahoy! Castaway ahoy!"

The shout from the crow's nest was loud and clear, even down in the mess hall.

"A-ha, sounds like we've spotted someone," said Comet. "Some poor hapless soul, cast adrift on a barren rock with their meagre possessions. They're lucky we've found them; I've heard of castaways going mad from loneliness, or getting so hungry they've been reduced to eating their own socks."

Sam gulped as he thought about his own parents stranded on the distant Planet X. *But they wouldn't have to eat their own socks,* Sam thought to himself. *They're both botanists, and they know everything there is to know about planets from all over the galaxy. They'll definitely be able to find food, even on a barren planet that's supposed to be made of gold. Won't they?*

Comet rose from the bench and interrupted Sam's thoughts. "Let's go and see who it is," he said.

Sam trooped up to the main deck with the crew, all eager to catch a glimpse of who the lookout had spotted. In the distance they could see someone waving from a large asteroid.

"Set a course for the asteroid please, Mr Pegg and Mr Legg," Comet called to the two-headed first mate who was steering the *Jolly Apollo*. Legg, the happier head, saluted sharply, while Pegg concentrated on the wheel.

The asteroid was small and round, barely big enough for a bowling lane, and piled high with suitcases. The castaway didn't seem too upset about being stranded. Leaning against a couple of his suitcases, he calmly waved to the approaching ship as if he didn't much care if they stopped or not. Sam frowned as he looked at him. The stowaway didn't look like he was marooned and desperate. He was wearing a gold-coloured cape over some pretty fancy pirate clothes and had a gold peg leg.

As the *Apollo* pulled alongside the stranger he tossed his head, flicking his wild black hair away from his face.

"Ahoy, me hearties!" he shouted in a deep voice. "What took you so long?"

"Ahoy!" called Comet. "Stand back, I'm coming down."

He dropped a rope ladder down to the asteroid and turned to Sam. "Rule fifty-six, paragraph three of the pirate code," he explained. "You always pick up a castaway. Now just watch his face when he realises he's been rescued by the famous Captain Joseph Hercules Invictus Comet!"

Sam held back a laugh. Comet rushed to put

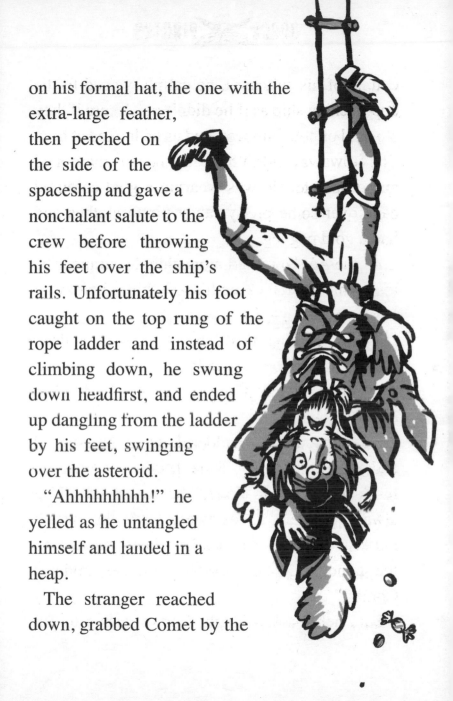

on his formal hat, the one with the extra-large feather, then perched on the side of the spaceship and gave a nonchalant salute to the crew before throwing his feet over the ship's rails. Unfortunately his foot caught on the top rung of the rope ladder and instead of climbing down, he swung down headfirst, and ended up dangling from the ladder by his feet, swinging over the asteroid.

"Ahhhhhhhhh!" he yelled as he untangled himself and landed in a heap.

The stranger reached down, grabbed Comet by the

scruff of the neck and hauled him to his feet.

Comet's hat was wedged down over his head and he wobbled around the asteroid as he struggled to get it off – much to the castaway's amusement. With one last mighty heave the hat flew off and Comet fell on his backside. The captain sat there blinking his one good eye in befuddlement. The stranger stared with a wry smile at the three-eyed pirate.

"There you go, Patches! Right way up again," said the stranger.

"Ah, erm, thank you," Comet replied, looking a bit flustered. He took a deep breath and puffed out his chest. "I'm Captain Com—"

"Be a good fellow," the stranger interrupted, "and grab those bags for me, will you? Getting up the ship's ladder is going to be a struggle with this."

He motioned to his golden peg leg, then gave Comet a wink and a pat on the cheek. "Make way, boys!" the stranger called up to the *Apollo*. "I'm coming aboard!"